"We love you, Clam and Sam!"

"Let's dance!"

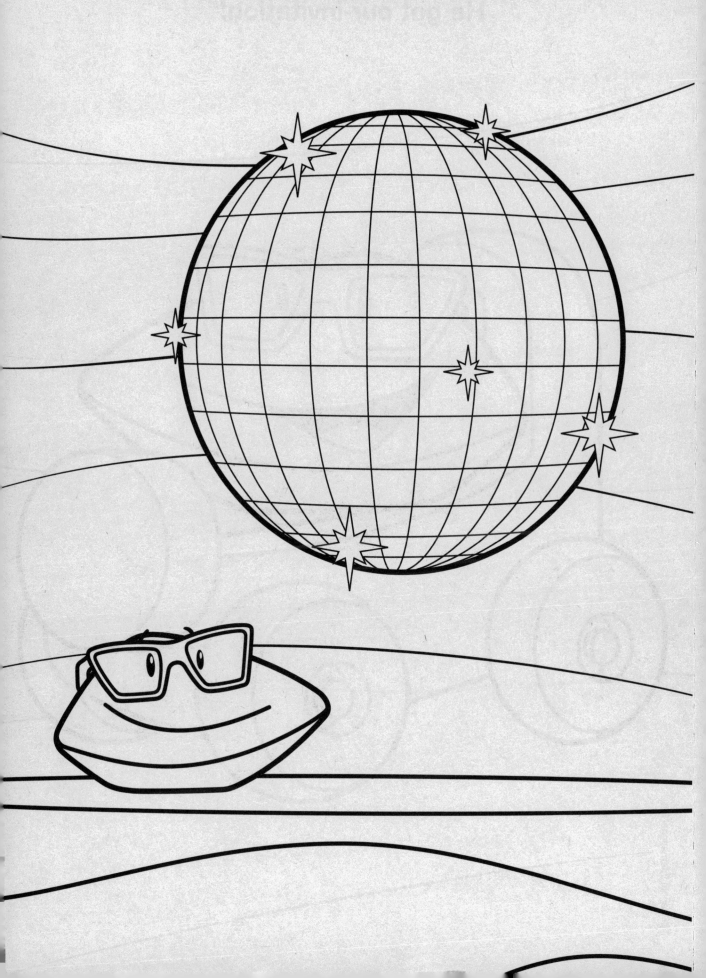

"Sam loves the disco ball!"

"There's a disco ball in the package!

"It's got a lot of stamps. That means it's really heavy!"

"I have some mail for Clam and the Bubble Guppies!"

"It's the mail truck!"

"I hear something. Is it Sam?"
Draw Sam inside Gil's thought bubble.

"I can't wait to dance!"

"We have some delicious snacks!"
Draw some apples and some orange slices for the party.

Draw some party hats
for Goby and Gil.

**"It's almost time for
the Happy Clam Day party!"**

"It's a *stamp*-ede!"

"A mail carrier had to watch out for grizzly bears and stampedes!"

**"In the old days, they used to deliver
mail on horseback."**

"Line up, everybody!"

"Line up, everybody!"

The oranges are heavier than feathers but lighter than a watermelon. Mr. Grouper needs four stamps.

Mr. Grouper wants to mail three oranges!
Draw them inside a package.

**There's a heavy watermelon
in Oona's package!
She needs six stamps.**

**Molly's package is light.
She needs two stamps.**

"Hello! I'd like to mail this package of feathers, please."

"Let's go to the post office!"

"You can send letters, packages, and postcards in the mail!"
Draw them in the bubbles.

"A *stamp*-wich!"

"Mail Carrier Nonny, what did you get for lunch?"

**"What time is it?
It's time for lunch!"**

"Let's sing a song about the mail!
La-la-letters!"

**"Then the mail carrier puts
the invitation in Sam's mailbox."**
Draw Sam's mailbox.

"Sam's mail carrier comes to pick up the invitation."

"The mail carrier drives the mail truck to the post office."

Decorate the post office.

"The mail carrier drives a mail truck."
Draw the tires on the mail truck.

"After you put the invitation in the mailbox, the mail carrier picks it up."

"First we need to put Sam's invitation in the mailbox!"

Draw a mailbox.

"Our invitation is ready to mail!"

"The sticker that goes in the corner of the envelope is called a stamp."

Draw a stamp for Sam's invitation.

"We need to write where Sam lives.
Sam's address is 6 Starfish Street."

Draw a 6 and a starfish on the envelope.

"We need to address the envelope."
Draw Sam on the envelope.

"Let's put the invitation in an envelope!"

Now it's time to decorate Sam's invitation!

"We'll send Sam an invitation in the mail!"
Draw an invitation for Sam inside the bubble.

"Let's have a Happy Clam Day party right here!"

"A party!"

"What happens on Happy Clam Day?"

"What happens on Happy Clam Day?"

**Clam wants to mail himself to his cousin
Sam for Happy Clam Day!**

The package is moving!
Clam is inside!

**Molly and Gil see a mailbox.
There is a package inside for them!**

BUBBLE PARTY!

**Great teamwork, Bubble Guppies!
You won the Crayon Prix! Your prize is . . .
A BIG, BEAUTIFUL BOX OF CRAYONS!**

And the winners are—
Team Guppy!

Will you help Molly and Deema race to the finish line?

Deema and Molly will do it!
Red and blue make purple!

Oh, no! Gil's car is sliding off the track!
Who will jump through the purple hoop?

Molly is zipping along the blue corkscrew!

Goby is shooting through the green loop!

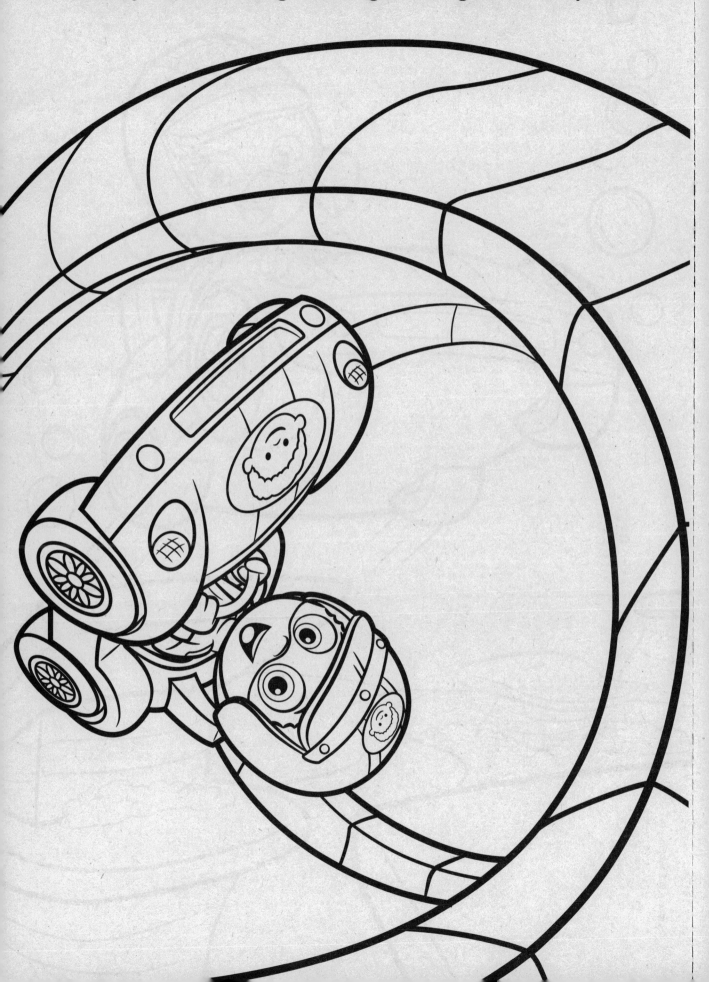

Oona is zooming off the yellow jump!

Nonny is crossing the orange bridge!

Deema is driving through the red tunnel!

Help the Guppies complete each Color Challenge!

"On your marks, get set . . ."

"Guppies,
start your engines!"

"Racers, to the starting line!"

"Now that we know our colors, it's time for the Crayon Prix!"

"Red means STOP!
Color the stop sign."

"Green on a traffic light means GO.
Color the bottom light green."

"Let's think about what colors can mean."

"Here we go!"
Vrooom!"

"We're ready to race!"

"This is your race car. What color do you want to make it?"

"Purple is my favorite color."

"I got a sandwich and a box
of *crayon*berry juice!"

"What time is it? It's time for lunch!"

"This is your helmet.
Decorate it with your favorite color."

Will you color Goby's helmet green?
Green is his favorite color!

"Let's color the helmets for our racers!"

"A rainbow has all the colors.
Will you color the rainbow?"

Oranges are orange—like Mr. Grouper!

"I like green.
Green is the color of frogs and peas."

"I want to choose my favorite color, but there are so many!"

Mr. Grouper says you can make any color by mixing red, blue, or yellow with other colors. Will you color the apple red, the blueberries blue, and the banana yellow?

**"Was there a purple race car, too?
Purple is my favorite color."**

"We saw a red car and a blue car."

"We saw race cars! They were really fast!"

Will you help Molly and Deema find the path to race to school?

START

FINISH

"I like the red race car!"

"Wait for the green light, racers! Green means GO!"

"Wow, it's a blue race car!"

"Deema, do you hear something?"

THE GREAT CRAYON RACE

"Cock-a-toodle-doo!"

What a great day on the farm!

Connect the dots to make a bell for Puddin'.

"Moo!"

"Hello, little calf. *Moo!*"

"What a wonderful surprise!"

**Connect the dots to finish
Butterscotch's trough.**

It's Butterscotch and her baby!

"I wonder what the surprise is!"

Help the Bubble Guppies find their way through the field back to the barn!

START

FINISH

"Farmer Joe has a surprise for us!"

Circle the tools that a farmer uses.

"A farmer works all day
to grow food for our meals."

"A farmhand is someone who helps a farmer."

"Farming is hard work."

How many pumpkins can you spot in the picture?

ANSWER: 5.

"Farmers also grow delicious, crunchy corn!"

"Make sure a bunny doesn't hop off with those carrots!"

"Those are some fine-looking carrots!"

"A farmer grows lots of vegetables—like carrots!"

"With sun and water, seeds grow into plants that feed you and me!"

Molly wants to water the plants.
Circle the tool she needs.

ANSWER:

"A farmer plants seeds in the ground and helps them grow."

Circle the chicken that is different.

ANSWER: C.

"*Cock-a-doodle-doo!*
A boy chicken is called a rooster."

"Chickens give us eggs."

Will you help the chickens get back to the coop?

START

FINISH

"Farmer Joe rides his tractor across the field."

"Hello, Farmer Joe!"

**"What animal says *'Cock-a-doodle-doo!'*?
A rooster!"**

Solve the maze to help Molly and Gil get to the farm.

START

FINISH

"Line up, everybody!"

"Let's go visit the farm!"

"There are horses and sheep on a farm."

"A farm animal that likes to roll around in the mud is called a . . . pig!"

"Let's think about it. Molly saw a cow."

"I want to see all the animals!"

"I want to go to the farm, too!"

Connect the baby animals to their mothers.

A

1

2

B

C

3

D

4

ANSWER: A-3; B-4; C-1; D-2.

© Viacom International Inc.

"I saw a cow!
And she's going to have a baby!"

"A *mooooose*?"

"*Moo!* Guess what I saw today, Mr. Grouper!"
Circle the animal Molly saw.

"Good morning, Mr. Grouper."

"Here are all my friends!"

"Here are all my friends!"

**"We made it to school.
C'mon inside!"**

Molly can't wait to tell her classmates about Butterscotch.

Help her find the path to school.

START

FINISH

"Moo!"
"Butterscotch likes the name Puddin'!"

"Hmm. . . . How about Puddin'?
Butterscotch and Puddin'!"

"What's the baby's name going to be, Farmer Joe?"

© Viacom International Inc.

Circle the two pictures of Butterscotch that are exactly the same.

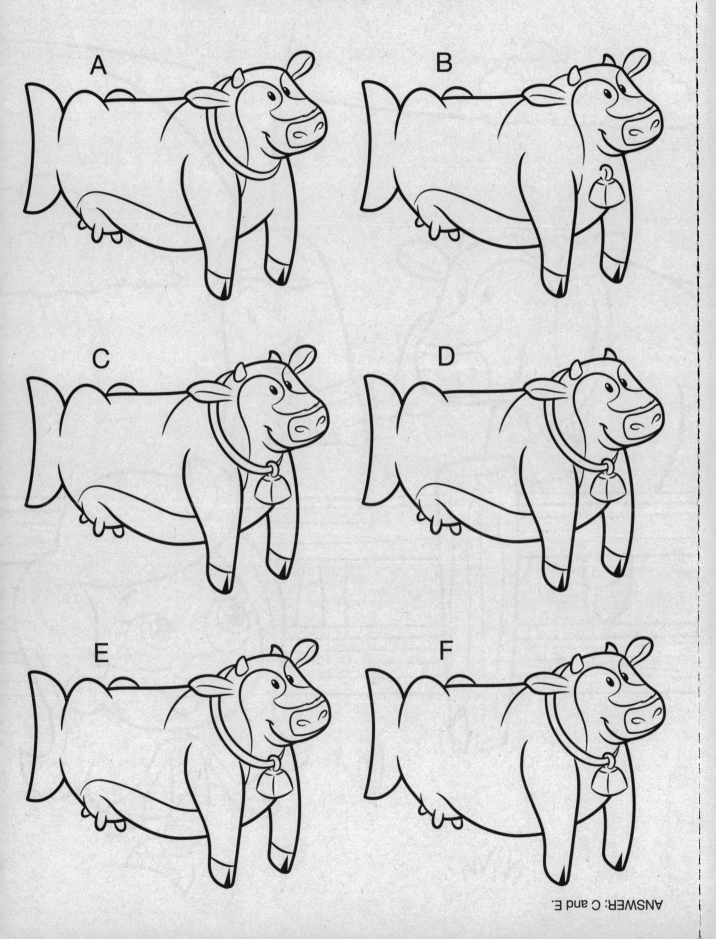

A

B

C

D

E

F

"Butterscotch is about to have a baby!"

"This cow's name is Butterscotch."

"Good morning, Farmer Joe!"

"Hello, cow!"

"Who's saying *'Moo!'*?"

"Hi! It's me, Molly!"

"Hi! It's me, Molly!"

ON THE FARM

"What a great day at school!"

"Look! I found some flowers for the class!"

"Playing outside at school is awesome!"

"C'mon and play!"

"It's time to go outside!"

"Line up, everybody!"

"I got a peanut butter and *smelly* sandwich?"

"I got a peanut butter and jelly sandwich."

"It's time for lunch!"

"It's time for lunch!"

"Excuse me, what time is it?"

"Class with Mr. Grouper is really super-duper!"

"I like story time."

"I love it when we get to . . . SIIIING!"

"I love it when we get to . . . SIIIING!"

"Do you like my picture
of a T. rex?"

"I like drawing pictures."

"Let's think about what we like best about school."

"We love our school!"

"Welcome to the classroom!"

"Good morning, Mr. Grouper."

Help Molly and Gil find their way to school.

START

FINISH

"C'mon! It's time to go to school!"

"We love Bubble Puppy!"

"Here, boy! Fetch!"

"Bubble Puppy loves to chase things!"

"Bubble Puppy can run really fast.
Whooooaaa!"

Help Gil find his way to Bubble Puppy.

START

FINISH

"This is Bubble Puppy."

"Arf! Arf!"

"I'm Nonny!"

"I'm Deema!"

"I'm Goby."

"I'm Gil!"

"I'm Molly!"

"It's time for Bubble Guppies!"

"What time is it?"

LET'S MAKE A SPLASH!

Illustrated by MJ Illustrations

Cover illustration colored by Steve Talkowski

A GOLDEN BOOK • NEW YORK

ISBN 978-0-385-37437-8
randomhouse.com/kids
Printed in the United States of America
10 9 8 7 6 5 4